ME

Other titles illustrated by Adrienne Kennaway
Baby Rhino's Escape
Bushbaby

Text copyright © 1998 Allan Frewin Jones

Illustrations copyright © 1998 Adrienne Kennaway

The moral rights of the author and the illustrator have been asserted

First published by Happy Cat Books, Bradfield, Essex CO11 2UT

A CIP catalogue record for this book is available from the British Library

ISBN 1 899248 47 1 Paperback
ISBN 1 899248 52 8 Hardback

Printed in Hong Kong by Wing King Tong Co. Ltd.

MEERKAT IN TROUBLE

ALLAN FREWIN JONES

ILLUSTRATED BY ADRIENNE KENNAWAY

Happy Cat Books

Mali the young meerkat lived with her family in the desert. She was old enough to take care of the baby meerkats but too young to go hunting with the grown-ups.

"Please can I come hunting with you now? It's boring here with the babies."

"No," said her mother. "You must watch over the young ones."

Mali was cross that she had to stay behind.

"Hooray!" shouted the babies. "Play with us, Mali, play with us."

Mali watched the hunting party leave.

"I'm just as clever as they are," she thought. "I could be a great hunter if only I was given the chance."

"I'm going out for a little while," Mali told the babies. "Stay here in the burrow until I get back."

"Where are you going?" they asked.

"Hunting," Mali called as she left.

What Mali didn't realise was that all the babies were following her!

Mali hadn't gone far when she came upon a family of lions asleep in the midday sun.

A young cub woke up. "Hello, there," he growled. "Who are you?"

"A meerkat. I was wondeing if meerkats eat lions," Mali said.

The cub growled and Mali quickly scampered off.

Mali tried to speak to a pair of antelope but they were running too fast to hear.

Then Mali saw a tortoise. "Could you tell me if there is any good food near here?"

"Plenty," said the tortoise. "Delicious grass and leaves and fungus."

"Meerkats don't eat those things," Mali said, and she went on.

"If you're hungry, I can show you where to dig for tasty roots,"
a porcupine told Mali. "And where to find fallen fruit."

"I don't think the babies would like that," Mali said.

"At last some proper meerkat food!" thought Mali as a
scorpion scuttled past. "But how can I catch it without
being stung?"

The baby meerkats couldn't keep up with Mali.
Where was she? They didn't know how to get back
to the burrow and they were quite lost.

"Lucky me," a cobra hissed, sliding towards the
frightened babies. "A tasty snack!"

"Mali!" the babies squealed. "Help!"

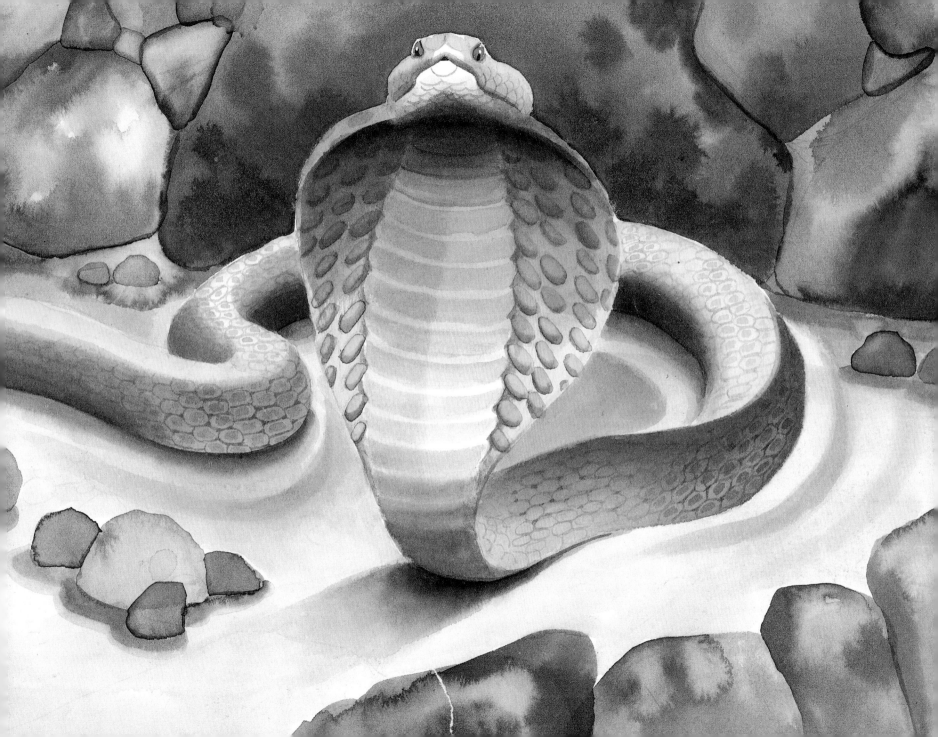

Mali heard the cries of the babies and came running.

"Slither off or I'll bite you really hard!" Mali screamed at the surprised cobra.

"Calm down," the snake hissed. "I'm going!"

"Follow me," Mali said to the babies. "We're going home."

Whoops! Mali led the babies straight over to a group
of young jackals.

"Nice of you to drop by," smiled a jackal. "Do stay
for lunch".

Laughing, the jackals crept nearer
and nearer to the little meerkats.

Suddenly the meerkat hunters appeared with angry cries.

"Run!" Mali's mother told the jackals, nipping them on the ankles. "There are more of us than you!"

Once they were all safely back at the burrow Mali's mother turned to Mali.

"You foolish meerkat," she said. "I asked you to take care of the babies."

"I'm sorry," Mali said. "I'll always do what I'm told in future."

"I should hope so!" her mother said.

But Mali wasn't in disgrace for long. That night the meerkats danced to celebrate their victory over the jackals and their safe return.

Because Mali had been so brave, she was allowed to lead the dance.

"And next time we go hunting," her mother said, "you can come with us."

"Yahoo!" Mali whooped, jumping for joy. "I'm the luckiest meerkat in the world!"

And that was probably true!